THE FIX IS IN

by

Robert Braithwaite

for Eunice

-CHAPTER ONE-

It wasn't often that Maurice Sheepshanks owned the sort of horse that was good enough to gallop with one of Lady Constance's. And when those rare days came round, it was less likely still that he was invited to watch them work, rather than her.

Francis Barrow went to greet him in the small car park behind his main yard. Leaning on the roof of Maurice's car as he spoke to him through its open window, he said, "They're already on their way down. Follow me."

Barrow set off across the car park, heading away from the yard and his offices, pausing briefly as he met the narrow path that meandered around the lunging rings, equine pool, and the back of the horse walker, to ask, "Good journey?" He didn't hear Maurice's reply as he pressed on, snaking through the hinterland of his operation. They eventually emerged into the no man's land by the groundsman's depot, where Maurice seized the chance to catch up with him, and repeat his answer about the journey. An enormous prefabricated metal barn dominated the space. They walked through it, heading for the open sliding doors at its far end where Barrow had built eight facing boxes in the dead space. As they were about to exit, one of his lads led out a horse from one of them, to put it on the walker. Maurice had just started to tell Barrow about the traffic on the M11, as Barrow paused for a moment to say, "That's going to be a very nice colt."

Maurice stopped talking, and paused to look at the passing horse. When he couldn't think of anything to say, he looked round for Barrow, hoping he might fill the silence, and saw him disappearing onto the path woven into the little wood that ran the length of the gallop —his calf length navy gabardine, and pomaded black hair, lending a vampiric air to his actions. The *home-ride* as Barrow's staff had learned to call it, comprised several parallel dolled-off strips of turf, with an all-weather piste at its far side, the fence of which, marked the southern boundary of Barrow's property. Maurice shed himself of his car coat, laying it over the side rails of a trailer, and set off in Barrow's wake.

As he emerged onto the grass verge of the home-ride, Barrow held up his finger, and said, "Stay there a moment." Then, he turned and walked on towards his assistant, Min Barker, who, having seen his intentions, came up to meet him.

"Ready?" said Barrow.

The question seemed to throw Min.

"Me, or err, them?" He pointed weakly over his shoulder.

"I'm dealing with them!" said Barrow. "Your thing —the video website whatsit."

"Oh, yeah, that. I am," said Min.

"Go on then," said Barrow. He took out his mobile phone, and held Min in his gaze as he did, until Min finally realised he was being asked to turn round, and head back to the place in which he'd been standing ready for the last twenty minutes.

Barrow still held the phone to his ear as he came back to pick up Maurice. He cut a slightly ridiculous figure, Maurice, with his flat cap, sleeveless argyle sweater, and binocular case neatly at his side on the end of a long diagonal strap, like a satchel. He wore large bifocals, which required him to tip his head backwards, as if looking down his nose, as people came into focus.

"You won't need them," said Barrow, pointing at Maurice's vintage binocular case. "Unless it's your packed lunch. They'll work between the three and the eight," he said. "Let's go up there a bit," pointing towards the elbow in the gallop. "No, not you!" he shouted into the phone. "Take another long turn, then you can come up."

As the horses galloped towards Min, crouching close to the six pole, the pacemaker gave way, and Maurice Sheepshanks' Astrakhan, took it up and stretched clear. Faithful rode Maurice's horse, and Squeezer, so named, not for his riding prowess, but because his face looked like it had been formed by having a lemon squeezer pushed through it from the back, sat in behind. As Faithful got down to ride his horse, Squeezer didn't move a muscle on Lady Constance's Lima.

Min couldn't see properly from his position, but it looked to him that Lima had pulled out and come upsides with Astrakhan as they reached the eight. It looked very different from Maurice Sheepshanks' angle.

"Crikey, he's good," he said, as Lima stretched past his horse in the final stages of the gallop. What's he rated?"

"Similar to yours, seventy–two," said Barrow. "Good worker, isn't he?"

They watched the horses pull-up and turn, then Barrow added, "I've got them in the same race at Leicester next week."

"Mine's seventy–nine —he'll never give him half a stone!" said Maurice. "We've got no chance."

"Really?" Barrow swung round to face Maurice, giving him a mock puzzled look, "I think you'll win." Maurice tried to conjure a response that conveyed, "That's obviously preposterous, because of what we both just witnessed." But before he could, he suddenly became aware of Min's presence.

"Yes?" said Barrow.

Min's slight frame, fresh face, shock of healthy hair, and good manners, saw him too often dismissed as a shy and irrelevant naif by people who didn't know him, when in fact, the opposite was true. They mistook his permanently curious expression for puzzled; the unmeant analytical stare, as betraying something docile; the moment's delay before he responded, an intellectual weakness.

"Sorry. I just wanted to know if..."

"Go and collect the horses," said Barrow, "and finish off the work properly." He rolled his eyes at Maurice, indifferent as to whether Min noticed or not. He did. No sooner had he set off on his way up the canter towards the horses, than Barrow's phone began to ring. It was Lady Constance. "Hold on," he shouted. Min turned, and Barrow tossed him his phone. "Deal with her, will you?" he said. Min's heart sank as he turned the phone to see the caller's name. He answered, and prayed he'd have the call finished by the time he reached the jockeys. She'd insist on talking to Squeezer, and Barrow would roast him alive if he let her.

"Give us yours then!" Barrow shouted after him. He strode over briskly to prevent Min from tossing it to him, snatched his phone, and turned back to Maurice. From over his shoulder, he called out, "You can finish that video thing on mine."

Faithful, the stable jockey, owed his nickname to another trainer who believed that the geyser, Old Faithful, was found in Faithful's native New Zealand. It had been meant as a compliment —that the jockey possessed an innate sense of timing that could be trusted to deliver without fail. "We went quick enough," he tried.

Squeezer nodded, then grunted, "Yeah, not bad."

"What start did you give us?" asked Faithful.

Squeezer gave him a look which said, "I've done my talking for the day."

"Come on. It'll be on the video," he said, indicating Min. "And the boss saw it. I'll know soon enough."

"See that last tree, on the other side?" said Squeezer. "When you hit the seven, I was still there." Faithful's leathery face turned white.

"Anything to say for the camera?" asked Min, and immediately regretted his naivety. The two old jockeys almost rustled a smile between them.

"I don't think the pacemaker went fast enough," said Faithful.

Min put his boss's phone to video, pointed it at the seven–furlong marker, and then at the horses, neither of whom were blowing. He let them go on, fell in behind, and continued to film until the horses turned left to go back to the yard.

He waited 'til the pacemaker, who had been tailed off in the work, went past him and back to the yard as the others had done. Then, with everyone out of sight, he headed back himself, taking the long way round, by the bottom of the home-ride, to eke out the time into a midday lunch break without any last-minute jobs falling his way. He knew that Barrow would be occupied with Maurice for a few minutes yet, and if anyone came looking for him, he could always claim to be picking up a horseshoe he saw lost in the work.

He thought better of his actions as soon as he arrived home, turned round, and drove straight back to the stables without getting out of his car. It just wasn't worth inviting the wrath of Barrow any more than he'd suffer it anyway, by hanging on to his phone. Maurice's car was still in the car park, and the outer door of the building containing Barrow's office was ajar. He went into the short corridor, and knocked on the closed door of Barrow's office. He heard noises inside, but nothing he could make out. He knocked again, and this time, he heard Barrow come quickly towards the door, and from a few paces away shout, "Go away!" through it, without asking who it was, or what it concerned. He left the phone leaning against the door frame, then changed his mind, just in case. Whatever he did, would be wrong, but a lost phone was a different level of grief, to a late-returned one.

Barrow didn't appear for evening stables. They bathed, massaged, medicated, and bandaged their horses, then, before the clock on the tower showed six, had them fed. As he walked past the office on the way home, he looked round the outer door, and saw a light under the door to Barrow's office. His heart sank, but knew that he must.

He knocked gently at the door, and this time he was invited in. Barrow sat at his desk, picking up and putting down documents as if he was searching for something he knew he'd seen recently. He stood as Min approached, still leafing through his papers as he did, the long tresses of his normally trained hair falling about his face. He waited until he was sure that Min had arrived at his desk, before looking up. "Ah, at last, my phone. Who's been on?"

Min didn't know, he'd put it on silent, and ignored it.

"You might have given me your code —that thing's been useless to me." He glanced down at the paper strewn desk, to a place where he thought he'd left it. Then he picked up his phone, and said, "Oh yes, Lady C.," before Min could properly explain that the reason he hadn't been able to give him the code, was entirely of his own making. Barrow called her number, without ending his conversation with Min, who stood mute, unsure whether he'd been dismissed, or was to wait until the call was finished. Barrow listened as she spoke, then after a minute or so, glanced up towards Min and said, "I don't know what gallop he was watching, but that's not what I saw." He smiled at her reply and shook his head gently.

"Don't be cheeky," he said, casting another brief glance at Min.

Min decided that it was time to go, and reached for the place he thought his phone might be lying, in the middle of the table. But, as he did, Barrow shooed him away with his free hand, wearing an expression that said, *don't you dare.* Min withdrew under the violence of the gesture, raising his hands to say, *I come in peace*, then, tentatively, ignoring all of Barrow's angry gesticulations, started searching among the papers and documents again, until he found his phone. Once he had, he held it up towards Barrow's face to show him what he'd done. But Barrow turned his gaze elsewhere as soon as he did, and went to stare out of the window, continuing his call as if Min was no longer there.

-CHAPTER TWO-

Min Barker poked his head around the door of the Tap House —one of three hundred or so similar pubs that claimed to be the oldest in England. There being no one worth avoiding, he committed to the entrance, and a pace or so away from the bar, he spotted Crab's suede leisure-shoe sticking out on the end of a spindly leg, from a booth in the far corner of the pub. He ordered two pints and took them into the little nook.

"I'm sorry," said Min. "I only picked up my phone at the end of the afternoon. I was, well, I'll tell you what I was, in a minute. It'll only sound like excuses now."

"Will it be worth waiting for?" asked Crab. Min nodded, smiling. "Anyway, what are you doing up here on a Thursday night?"

"I am fair-ing le pont, Min, that's what I'm doing."

"You're what-ing the what?"

"I had to take a day off today, so I added another tomorrow to make a long weekend of it."

"Since when have you started doing things like taking days off?" asked Min.

"Since I learnt about holiday allowances. Apparently, you get thirty days a year. Did you know about all that?"

"Yes," said Min. "Of course I did. Everyone does."

"I didn't," said Crab. "I thought it was two weeks annual leave, and corporate jollies, until about a month ago. I wish you'd told me."

Min laughed. "So, you're kicking-back, eh? I thought you were looking a bit Dubai."

"Get used to the new me," said Crab. "Oh yes, speaking of which, are you..."

Min cut him off. "Before you ask. No! I am not available for playing out. I work in horse racing, even our weekends-off include working on Saturday mornings."

"What about Saturday night? I was planning to take you two country bumpkins out for a bit of nosebag. I can keep the lovely Jane company 'til you de-fumigate yourself."

"I mightn't be home 'til midnight from Haydock, and I'm working Sunday." Min stopped himself from saying more, and took a long draught of his beer.

Crab did the same. "What's the matter? Tell uncle."

"Nothing. I'm fine," said Min, diverting his gaze from Crab.

"You could tell your face that. The fight with the old ennui seems to be in vain, my friend."
Min sighed resignedly, as if to say, *ok, you asked*. Then he began: "You know how in the City, everyone is utterly venal, aggressive, and sort of stupid?"

Crab nodded encouragingly.

"Well, racing's like that, but with ignorant thrown-in too. Barrow doesn't even pretend that he's not treating you like a slave. And the demeaning tasks you have to perform to keep owners onside, or get them to buy a new horse! Dear me. I just thought that for once I'd have a job where I didn't feel like a greasy salesman."

"You have one of the most oleaginous sycophants in the Square Mile sat opposite you. It's not all bad."

"Yeah, well, working for Barrow, I feel like a prostitute. And on the days when you've had enough, there's no one to go and bitch to. There isn't a good one amongst them. I don't know why they send criminals to prison —they should send them to work in racing stables. They are the most compassionless dens of sociopaths and ne'er do wells that the world has ever invented."

"Look, I can't come up every week. It's given me an attack of hives to take Friday off when I didn't need to."

Min smiled weakly, perhaps in mourning for his old life. "I feel like one of those idiots who went somewhere on holiday, and decided to live there. Today right, the thing I'm going to tell you about, he made me take the call from Lady Constance, which was the usual nightmare by the way,"

"I believe so," said Crab.

"Believe what?" asked Min.

"Lady thingy. Her old man. Her former old man, I should say. He's on the board at our place now. He's a racing nut. A steward, I think, too. Whatever. He's quite connected. We've become sort of mates, me and Sir Michael. You know —united by a love of the turf. I love it when he comes to meetings, we don't do any work" he said, emphasising the *am*. "She sounds like a disaster. Apparently, she's as nutty as a fruit cake —always ringing up trainers at all times of the day and night. Takes her horses away on a whim, then sends them back a week later."

Min cut across him. "I know. I'm one of the people she rings up. Anyway, back to my story —while I was speaking to her, Barrow took my phone. When eventually he let me back in his office, he bollocked me because he didn't know my PIN and hadn't been able to use it. He took his back, rang her, then proceeded to contradict every single thing that I'd told her —I'd hedged my bets with her, because I know what he's like, but he was all: "I don't know what gallop he was watching." Right in front of me, Crab! He doesn't even comprehend that there'll be consequences for him by undermining me —I mean, why would she ever want to speak to me again? Mind you, I think he's knocking her off, which would put a slightly different dynamic on it all, I suppose. Jesus, you should hear him trying to show his lighter side, it's like listening to an AI Bot, telling a dirty joke."

"What does Jane say about it all?"

"Please don't mention any of this to Jane, she'd lay an egg. She's only just adjusted to this place —and she thinks I'm happy!

"The poor deluded thing." Crab took a sip from his drink, and screwed up his face. "You have got it bad, haven't you?" he said, sniffing the beer. He held his drink up to the light, then inspected the branding on the glass.

"I'm getting close to the end of the breathing space I gave myself, I will say that," said Min.

"What's the deadline?" asked Crab.

Min sipped his beer. "My final bonus payment is all but gone. Once it has, it's going to be all too apparent what an error this was," he glanced briefly at the floor. "And don't say that to Jane, either."

"Schtum," said Crab, and gave him the Scout salute. "So, you're thinking of leaving? You could probably get a similar job back, you know. In a much worse place, of course, but still, insurance never goes out of fashion."

Min laughed. "Crab, you are such a comfort. Never thought of a job in racing yourself? You'd fit right in. And I didn't say that. I'm not quite there yet."

Crab took a slurp of his beer, and put it to one side as if that would be his last. "Do you recall what we say when we encounter people like you in meetings?

Min shook his head.

We say, 'I'm confused.' Then we follow that up with something that makes you look like an imbecile. Though in this case, I don't think I need bother. Are you staying, or going? Which is it?"

"Staying. For now. Because of what I'm about to tell you."

Min pulled his chair closer to the table, looked left for enemy combatants, then leaned in to his friend.

"Just a minute," said Crab. "This feels like it's going to be at least a pint's worth of anecdote. Fresh one?"

He pushed back his chair, rose up, crouched to prevent his head from touching the ceiling, then shuffled out sideways from the tight space to the bar —an action which had not given him his nickname; nor was it for the fact that he always got his round in last; and it was only in part because of his complexion, which, where it was not pink, was white. No, Crab had been given his name for the way he behaved when in drink —his six foot–three willowy frame, suddenly incapable of supporting its own weight, saw him bend to and fro, as if he had no backbone, like a crab stick held at the bottom, someone once observed. Overnight, he left Stick behind forever, spent a few weeks as Crab Stick, then turned into Crab, which he'd remained ever since. Min checked his phone as he waited, and smiled to himself.

When Crab returned, Min embarked on the story which was still forming in his head. He began with the gallop he'd watched earlier that morning, telling Crab, how he'd arrived unseen, and heard Barrow say to Maurice, "Really? I think you'll win."

He raised up his hands to request that he be allowed to continue without interruption. "You'll know when you've seen the video of the gallop," he said, anticipating Crab's objection. "You had to hear it Crab, the way he said it. Even from the angle on the video, once you've watched it a couple of times, that vacant, lost-for-words expression Maurice threw at me suddenly made sense." He told Crab again about how his and Barrow's phones had come to be swapped; how the video he was recording was left running as Barrow took his phone; and how Barrow could do nothing about it, because he didn't have the screensaver PIN.

"For the first five minutes or so, it sounded like a… you know, that thing. It's got a name."

"A butt call," said Crab. "And let that be the last Americanism uttered today," he added.

"Then, once they'd got back to the office, the phone seemed to have been dropped onto Barrow's desk, with both men sat roughly opposite. They'd wandered about a bit," he told Crab, "and went in and out of the range of the phone. But you can sort of fill in most of the gaps with intelligent guesses."

"Maurice had said something. It doesn't matter what. The answer's the important bit. Barrow just shot a reply back at him, saying something like, 'Yes, but did you see how he *dropped the lot* as soon as he got in front?' he told Crab."

Crab nodded sagely.

Min continued. "He kept saying that Lima was a very smart horse, but he kept using this same phrase — that his jockey would have to learn to *finesse him*. You know, as if Lima could be one of those horses that stop racing as soon as they got in front, and have to be produced right on the line, to prevent them from throwing it away."

"Yes, I know what finesse means," said Crab. "Is he?"

"Lima?" said Min. "Anything but. He always finishes off his work really well, and the one time he raced, in that maiden, he just destroyed them. I mean, the rest were all useless, but he didn't look like he stopped racing when he went past them that day."

Crab shrugged, cueing Min to continue.

"So, once he'd got that idea into Maurice, he started talking about Astrakhan being a more honest type."

Min said he'd listened to the main parts of the conversation three or four times now. He described the layout of Barrow's office to Crab, and set a scene where Barrow walked all around it, hands clasped behind his back, like an attorney making his rehearsed speech appear as if he was making it up as he went along.

He looked at Crab to check that he was engaged, and received a smile in return, which seemed to say, *I'm indulging you, and I'm tolerating this. For now.*

"Sorry, I digressed. So next he goes, 'You know that the whole world knows that Lima's the better horse, don't you?' You could sense that Maurice sort of bristled. Then once he had him cornered, he went for it, 'See who rode the work? Jockeys like Squeezer, they've all got gamblers behind them. And he works for them, not for me. And they definitely don't work for you. It's good practice to have them get their fingers burned every now and again,' Maurice took it all in silence, but I can picture his confused little face, following Barrow round the room, like he was watching a bluebottle buzzing round his head."

Crab remained silent. He was either concentrating, or could no longer look Min in the eye.

Min ignored him and continued. "It went a bit faint then, as if Barrow had turned his back on the phone, but he seemed just to repeat some of his stock phrases, you know, vague, condescending things that people like him use to try and extract loyalty from their subjects, like, who do you want to win? Them or us? I can't remember what it was, but it felt like something used to fill the silence, and perhaps provoke a response from Maurice. Well, shortly afterwards it did, and Maurice comes in loud and clear saying, 'Yeah, but we both saw what happened this morning —the other horse is simply miles better than mine.' That's when it got interesting," said Min.

"You don't say," said Crab.

Min stuck his head out into the bar to check if they could be overheard, then beckoned Crab to the far end of the little alcove. He adjusted the volume on his phone, so that only they, fully concentrating, could hear it. Then he pressed play. "Listen for yourself," he said.

Barrow's clipped, army-polished, boarding school English could be heard first. "We'll need a pacemaker," he said. And there was something almost derisive in Maurice's reply. It was muffled, but they could detect indignation in his voice, "But that would make Lima's job even easier," he said. Min and Crab shrugged at each other to say, *you can't argue with that.*

"You don't understand what I'm saying," said Barrow. His voice was much clearer. As if he was closest to the phone.

"He'd fit in well in one of our meetings," said Crab, smirking.

Min shushed him curtly, and Crab did as he was told.

As they tuned in again, Barrow was explaining to Maurice that he was suggesting a different kind of pacemaker to the one Maurice had in mind —one that got in front, then slowed it all right down, to stack up the field behind. Then there followed a sudden noise, that sounded like thrashing about. Min laughed, as he had on previous listenings when he reached this part, imagining little Maurice struggling to get out of the armchair, angry, and anxious to make his point.

"Well, then the others will go on," he said eventually.

When Barrow replied "Will they?" a theatrical wink could almost be detected in his voice.

"In that case," said Maurice, coming as close as Barrow to the phone, 'If they lob round in a bunch, and have a sprint over the final furlong, Lima's class will be even more telling.'

Crab was as engaged as Min now, and he dipped his head closer to Min's phone.

"That's right," said Barrow. "Correct."

He seemed to stroll around his desk, then take a prolonged look out of the window, pondering all the possibilities before he delivered his smoking gun evidence. When he came back to the desk, he said, "But what if he doesn't get out in time?" He paused for a second for the point to land with Maurice, then added, "Or more to the point, panics and goes too soon?"

"What's he like, this Maurice?" asked Crab.

Min, sighed, pausing the video, "How should I put it? He's terribly earnest. Think of Tweedle Dee and Tweedle Dum, with their little pot bellies, about four foot tall, staring at the world from under their school caps. That's him —with this sort of obstinate, belligerent, way about him. He professes to demand absolute honesty from everyone he meets, but if you pay lip service to that, he's like a lap dog, and will believe anything you tell him. Deferential I suppose —sort of in awe of Barrow. But there's something else about him too. He's, err, lacking. That's it," he said. "He is handicapped by a lack of imagination."

"Sounds impressive," said Crab.

"Very much so," said Min. He restarted the video.

"He's a horse that needs to be finessed, remember," said Barrow. You could almost hear the penny drop with Maurice.

Min and Crab looked at each other in faux-shock, their jaws dropped. Eventually, Min said, "So, Maurice realises that Barrow's trying to describe a race set up for him to win. He gets it. Let's not keep listening in here, my heart's in my mouth." He stopped the video and put his phone away.

"Anyway, eventually, after he's finally processed what's being proposed, he goes, 'What are you going to do? Enter six horses?' And Barrow, who as you know, is congenitally incapable of so much as hearing a criticism against him, instead of taking offence, just started laughing."

Crab smiled encouragingly. Min took a long draught of beer. "Ooh that's a bit better," he said. Crab widened his smile, and nodded, as if to say, *I know*. Min went on.

"Then there's another long silence, but eventually, Barrow says, 'You understand as much about this as I do, Maurice, six is the magic number.' To Maurice's obviously confused expression, he explained, 'With six horses, in those sort of races, we can guarantee most outcomes. But we don't need to own all the horses —just the drivers.' Then he repeated another of his nonsense platitudes, like, 'There's no I in team,' whatever that's supposed to mean."

"I know," said Crab, "Why do people say that? It's ridiculous. Like a word is invalidated if it happens to include a smaller word within it, that hints at the opposite? What's that all about?"

"And there's a *me,* in it," said Min.

"Oh yeah, I never thought of that. It doesn't even work on their own terms. That makes it even worse! I'm going to adopt that from now on. Every time some bore tries to get their own way by evoking a non-existent team spirit, that's totally alien to them, and they say *there's no I in team*, I'm going to reply, "Yeah, but there's a me in it. It's great that, I love it. Are you sure you don't want to come back? The meetings are going to improve out of all recognition."

"Ooh, feeling a bit raw, are we? It sounds like you've been rumbled lying on your CV again," said Min, laughing.

"What?" said Crab.

"Team player, self-starter," said Min. "You haven't dropped your guard, and allowed them to realise that you're obnoxious and selfish, have you?"

"Err, strongly personally motivated, if you don't mind," said Crab. "And no. I'm a delight. I just have a secret desire to vanquish all the Barrows in my life. It is a bit smelly though, isn't it? Not that team thing —Barrow's scheming."

"Oh, that's right! Maurice said something similar. Smelly, I mean —you know that thing he has about being a straight-dealer. He started talking about the other owner, saying he wouldn't like to be stitched up like that, but Barrow just jumped in and said, 'It'll help Lima's handicap mark,' in a way that you could tell that he couldn't care less what the horse's handicap mark was. Don't worry about the other owner, he said They'll get their turn. That's about it," said Min. "What do you think?"

Crab screwed up his face, "You want my advice as a neglectful and lazy financial advisor, or a recidivist Turfiste?"

"What's the difference?"

"Fair point. It's very beguiling, Min. And there's something up, obviously. It stinks, it really does. And there's a plan afoot, but, for me, it raises more questions than answers. Have you stumbled across version-one of the plan, which will change next week, and the week after; or was he setting up Maurice? Or you, perhaps? How does it work? How many people need fixing? Have they done it before? If so, with whom? Who puts the money on? Whose money, is it? Wanting it to be true is very tempting, but it's a very dangerous thing, Min."

"Well, it's not about setting me up —you should hear what he says about me, at the end. And he's got them both in the same race at Leicester at the end of next week."

"To be honest, I'd like to hear it all again. In the peace and quiet," said Crab.

"I'll send it to you from my home Wi-Fi," said Min. "Oh yeah, one last thing. Once Maurice had come to terms with the plan, he started asking about the payback, and whether it would compromise him, and his horse, and all that sort of thing. Guess what Barrow said? He goes, 'Make the most of it, you'll never beat him again.' Now, that to me underlines it all in ink. And, what's even better —we now know that they've got the best horse up their sleeve for next time!"

"It could make the weekend go with a bang if it all works, I suppose," said Crab. "But it's the logistics I want to think about. As we say in insurance, it's never about the idea in the end; it's always about the execution. Do you know when he might have done it previously?" he asked.

"No. I was planning to research all that tonight, had I not started drinking beer with you. What weekend?" asked Min.

Crab drained his pint, banged the empty glass on the table in request of another, and shouted, "Aubergiste!"

Min shushed him again.

"Jesus, Min! The stag-hen thing. You and Jane, me and The Mistress, and perm any two of the three Donahue sisters. My stag! Of which you are Best Man, even though I'm doing all the organising. The one where we eschew the norms, have a gastro weekend in Paris, mano a womano. Let the Montrachet flow like a river in spring, we said."

Min swigged off his beer. "When did I agree to this?"

"You didn't. Well, you did. I'm here to confirm. I mean, to tell you I'm collecting the deposits. And then to, err, collect them, I suppose. Get us some pork scratchies, will you?"

"You're going on a before-the-wedding honeymoon, and taking your friends?"

"Something like that. Oh, I see your confusion. Don't worry, she doesn't get a cooling-off period with the prenup."

"That's a relief," said Min. "What weekend?" he gathered the empty glasses.

"The French Derby! First Sunday in June. You know, how Jane has never seen it —the race that is, not Paris. Well, it's Chantille actually, but we're stopping in Paris. How you promised her? Springtime in Paris and all that. Or is it autumn?

"That's only five weeks away," said Min standing up. "I'll be busy here. I can't book that time off."

"You can and you will. If not for me, then for Jane."

Min stopped on the way to the bar, "Does she even know about it? Has Eleanor told her?"

Crab shrugged

When he returned with the beer, he said, "Alright. But can I give you the deposit after Leicester?

"Provided you've booked the time off by then, of course. I'll cover it."

"And are you coming to Leicester?"

"Now, that's a definite yes," said Crab. "Even if I have to squander another day's holiday on it."

-CHAPTER THREE-

Logistics. It was the last word uttered by Crab to Min, as he left the stands to prepare his horse. He was to lead up Astrakhan, ridden by Faithful. They were firm in their convictions that something was up, but the *how-to's* of it all, still remained a mystery.

"You're brave," said Faithful, as Min led him round. Min shot him a confused look, and Faithful explained, "Volunteering for a race like this."

"I don't mind giving up my Saturdays," said Min.

Faithful smirked. They were in the paddock early. Min had asked Faithful a favour to weigh out before the previous race, so that they could do a couple of laps of the paddock, and have Astrakhan dispatched to the start as soon as the rest of the field started to arrive.

They walked towards the chute that led out to the course, and Faithful said, "Do one more, there's no one here. We don't want to draw attention." Min obliged, and then, half a dozen strides or so later, Faithful added, "You'll still have time to get your money on." He looked straight ahead as he said it, inviting no reply. Min's stomach dropped as he stole a look at the jockey. Was it judgmental, or in jest? Maybe he was just testing him?

That's when it happened. Two horses came into the paddock together, and one of them was skittish, and was a handful for his lass. He wouldn't settle, and his trainer decided to deal with the situation by getting him jocked-up, and sent early to the start. Min and Faithful timed their own walk round the paddock to keep the horse at the greatest distance from them. But then, the horse threw his young jockey and, once free, went bucking and kicking round the paddock. People scattered, and Astrakhan got up on his toes. Min clung onto him for dear life, not sure whether he should retreat to a far corner, or to make for the chute, to get him and Faithful away onto the safety of the course.

Only Barrow ran towards the paddock. "What are you doing here?" He shouted. "Get him back in the pre-parade, away from these amateurs."

The subject sort of broached, once they were back in the quiet of the pre-parade, killing time until the incident was resolved, Min attempted to delve further. A sort of tentative trust had been established between him and Faithful, but it was early days still, and the wrong question, or the right question poorly pitched, would reveal his status as the eavesdropper, trying to inveigle his way into the action. "Will it change the plans, if the horse is withdrawn?" he tried.

"Doubt it, it's only the rag," said Faithful screwing up his face.

They walked on in silence, as Min dredged his mind for a relevant rejoinder to keep the conversation alive. But none came. They, and two other horses, walked round the pre-parade. The other four remained behind the scenes still. It was an empty and desolate scene. Small talk seemed inappropriate.

A lap and a half of the little pre-parade ring had been endured in a strained silence, when Faithful, standing up in his irons to steal a view of the main paddock, said, "They've caught it, look —no damage done." Then he added, "Oh yes there is. That boy's still down. The medics are with him." He sat back into his saddle again, then added, "So, all they've got to do, is find another mug to ride it." Then he laughed his head off, as if he'd told the funniest joke anyone had ever heard.

Barrow arrived while he was still chuckling to himself, and immediately ordered Faithful down from the horse. "You're supposed to be looking after it, for God's sake!" he said. "The race could be ten minutes delayed yet!" He looked at Min as if to say, "Why didn't you tell him that?" shook his head, then left, without another word.

"Is this our bonding moment?" thought Min, catching Faithful directly in his eye for a fleeting moment, as they shuffled into their positions for the remaining laps of the pre-parade.

"The horse is alright, did you say?" he tried.

"They'll want it to run. It makes up the dead eight runners," said Faithful.

"Dead eight?" said Min, almost whispering. "They don't back them each-way, do they? Why bother?" And he immediately regretted pitching his question in the third person, instead of finding a way to ask it that implied he was an integral part of the scheme.

"Who knows what plans they have?" said Faithful, "They might. The people backing the horses probably don't even know yet." He sort of nodded towards the betting ring, as he said it, as if the people charged with betting the horses were present at the track, and known to him.

It prompted the next question for Min, from where their conversation picked up from its faltering, staccato. Whether Faithful was put out at receiving a dressing down, was bored waiting for the hold up to be cleared, or became more garrulous as soon as he knew he was away from prying ears, he suddenly seemed prepared to chat. Perhaps he believed that he was talking with someone on the inside of the coup. Whatever the motivation, he began to talk to Min as if they were colleagues who found themselves on the same side of the deal.

For his part, Min tried to commit it all to memory as he fed Faithful his cues for each next building block in the story.

He relayed all he could remember to Crab when he met him at the paddock gate to the racecourse a few minutes later. "Listen Crab," he said, "I am just going to brain dump it all on you. Don't interrupt 'til I stop."

Crab nodded earnestly.

"OK. The number one rule, above all others: cash only!"

"What?" said Crab. "They bet in cash? Who does that? Who even carries cash?"

Min shushed him. They weren't clear from the hubbub of people and horses yet, and did not know who might overhear their conversation. "I thought I asked you not to interrupt? It's how they manage compliance," said Min in a forced whisper. "I'll tell you all about it on the way. But we'd better go and find ourselves a cash machine, before we do anything else."

The last horse to leave the paddock passed them on the chute.

"It's ridiculous," said Crab, "I've only got a hundred or so."

"I've got even less," said Min. "Come on. It's not worth being on the wrong end of them, believe me."

They walked and jogged as they searched for an ATM machine, eventually finding one in the lobby of the main hall by the entrance to the racecourse. Four other people queued ahead of them. Without any discussion, they decided as one to take their medicine, and took their place at the end of the line. They looked up at the screen which would later show the race, and saw that the horses were already circling at the start.

"So, what are the consequences of non-compliance?" asked Crab.

"For the jockeys, especially the young ones, no more rides. They just dry up."

"That can't be right," said Crab. "How do they have such reach?"

"I don't know whether Faithful was mythologising it all —but he didn't sound like he was," said Min. "I guess he's talking about those gambling owners with big strings —they exert a lot of influence. I suppose they provide the majority of rides for some riders on the way up. Anyway, and these are his words, he described it all as an *invitation only club, with a regular pay-day.* 'We just do our jobs and keep our heads down,' he said. I asked him whether it had always been like that, and he goes, 'Remember the Boy Scout?' I said, 'Yes, he was one of my favourite jockeys, what happened to him?' and Faithful just said, 'Precisely.' Scary, eh? Do you remember how he just disappeared?"

The racecourse announcer came in, "They're going behind."

They were next in the queue.

"Anyway," said Min, "He'd taken me into his confidence, so I said, 'I'm surprised Squeezer's involved. He's got his own following —they could spoil the whole thing."

"God, No wonder you were no good at insurance," said Crab, barely concentrating.

Min ignored him, he knew his attention was elsewhere, and went on with his story, "So, Faithful then said, 'Yeah, but he isn't winning.' Min looked for a reaction from Crab, but none came. So, I replied, 'But if he's going to get beat, he'll have told that to his followers too —it amounts to the same thing to them.' Guess what he said?"

Crab's eyes bored into the back of the head of the woman in front, as she cancelled her transaction, and began again. She seemed almost certain to spontaneously combust under the intense, impatient fury he channelled at her.

Min continued regardless, "He said, 'Squeezer? He doesn't know yet.' I mean, two minutes before the race, and he still doesn't know that he's going to be told to come second, and set the race up for the other horse. I asked when he would find out, and Faithful said, 'When Barrow takes him, to leg him up.' Can you believe it?" Crab turned to Min in an attempt to find a distraction so that he might contain his anger. "What?"

"What, what?" said Min.

"Your story," he said. "What are you wittering on about? I can't tell which *he* was who, and what *him* was someone else."

Min exhaled audibly, "I was telling you what Faithful told me about Squeezer —that he won't know that he's not going to win, until Barrow takes him to leg him up on the horse."

The woman in front of them, shouted, "Don't tell me!" at the screen, then went into her purse for a new card. Crab's features tightened again. He dipped his head to stare at the floor, and reset his breathing to long, slow and deliberate lungfuls of air.

Before he was fully recomposed, Min nudged him, and pointed to the betting boards, which showed that Astrakhan had drifted to ten–to–one; and Lima was fifteen–to–eight.

The first horse was being led in.

The woman's second card didn't work. She turned round to Crab and said, "It doesn't do fivers."

"How much do you want?" asked Crab.

"Twenty–five quid," she said.

"If you let me go next, I'll give you thirty," said Crab nodding to encourage her into the transaction. "How's that?"

"Are you sure?" she asked.

"Certain," he said making a circling gesture with his index finger towards his head. "But remember my face. One day, I might need a favour back."

They did the transaction with the woman, got their cash, and saw that there were only four horses left to load.

"We'll never get there in time," said Crab, rooting himself to the spot. "Let's get some on with our phones, no one will notice at this late stage."

Min looked up at the boards. Astrakhan was at twelves. "They haven't started gambling him yet. There's still time," he said.

"How do you know?" asked Crab.

"They back Lima, to lead a false trail, and then, at the last minute, they have their real bet on the other one, which by then will have drifted to a good price."

"Crafty," said Crab. "And quite smart —they get a bit of insurance that way too, in case it all goes wrong."

"Yes," said Min, urging him forward. "We'll do all the theory later. Now, we have to get the money on."

"Come on, let's just do it on the phones. No one will know," said Crab.

Min dragged him on, out of the hall. "They will! They will notice that someone has taken the best of their price. And they'll know that we're here asking questions, taking an unhealthy interest. It won't take them long to put us on their shortlist. God, Crab —they're shrewd. Please, listen to me; be reasonable. It's the first time we've done this. We're still finding out how it all works. Let's at least play by the rules that we've only just learned. There's still Lima to come next time, and we'll know how they do it then. Please."

The racecourse announcer came in, "Just having a little trouble getting Vino de Vici in. He got himself into a bit of a tizz in the paddock, and he's proving no less difficult for his young jockey here."

Crab nodded his consent, and picked up the pace. As the ring came into view, pausing between spurts of jogging to regain his breath, he asked, "What do think happens to people like us if we're discovered? We won't be sent to Siberia like those poor young boys?"

- 34 -

"No, it's much worse than that," said Min, walking on as he talked, to encourage Crab to do the same.

"What then?" asked Crab, "Not fisticuffs?" He went white as he contemplated the words that had just fallen from his mouth.

"Even worse," said Min, tugging at Crab's jacket. "According to Faithful, they disappear you from your money."

"The absolute savages," said Crab, slipping his phone back into his breast pocket.

As they arrived at the edge of the betting ring, the bookmaker chalked off Astrakhan's price, and replaced it with a nine.

"They've started," said Crab. "And we've missed the best of it already."

"I can't be seen betting —you do it," said Min. "But don't get in their way!"

"How will I know which they is *them*?" asked Crab.

"Just go," said Min. "Use your initiative."

The commentator announced, "Just one to go now."

"It's too late. We'll have to do it on our phones," said Crab. "They've already taken the best of the price. They won't mind."

"Give me your phone," said Min impatiently. "I'll do a bit, while you get the cash on. But only a bit," he stressed. "Something that won't be noticed. Go on, do as much as you can with the cash, while we still can."

Crab opened his phone, swiped his fingerprint password, and gave it to Min. Then he spun on his heel, and sped off towards the betting ring, his arms and legs thrown to the air in random gestures towards athleticism, like a ventriloquist's doll escaping from his master. Min raised his eyebrows at no one in particular, and jogged off to the low steps of the grandstand.

When Crab joined him, breathless, a few moments later, he said, "I didn't get it all on. Some of the bookies had taken too much on the horse already, and wouldn't take a bet at any price. There's still all this left," he said, showing Min a handful of cash. We've got to put the balance on with our phones now. Barrow's lot have had their bet."

Min was still reluctant. The stories he'd heard from Faithful revealed a real menace, which he'd been unable to convey in quite the same way when he'd repeated them to Crab.

"The price has already dried up —it can't spoil it further," Crab pleaded.

"They're about ready," said the course commentator.

"I'll tell you what we'll do," said Min. "When the gates have opened, and the race has started, we'll get as much as we want on, on the betting exchanges. We can't spoil their price then."

"And they're off!"

Min looked up at Crab as the horses hit the furlong post. "Eleven—to—two," he said, dejectedly.

"Me too," said Crab.

They shook their heads at each other. Both agreed that they could not have made a worse job of getting their share of the bet on. The adrenalin suddenly gone, cold hard reality set back in. "I've had more on than I meant to, all at a worse price than anyone else who's backed the horse," said Min.

"It could yet be worse," said Crab. "I'm still not entirely sure we've backed the right one."

They turned their attention to the race, and saw that the pacemaker had taken an uncontested lead, and lobbed along steadily, one lane out from the rail. Astrakhan sat about a length and a half behind him, tight on the rail, with Lima about three—quarters of a length behind Astrakhan, on his outer. Another horse, on Lima's outside, was about a neck in front of him, making a sandwich of him with Astrakhan. Vino di Vici was unsuited by the slow early pace, and would not settle. Throughout the early stages, he looked certain to run away with his inexperienced rider and have his race done before half way. But to the young girl's credit, by the time they passed the two—marker, she had her horse's head buried in Lima's tail, where he was suddenly in love with life again. Until that moment, a frisson of anxiety had run through the field of jockeys, each of them suddenly forced to think about how they'd improvise the agreed plan, if Vino di Vici had got free.

Just after the three–pole, the pacemaker's rider injected a little pace, and in the stands, and the commentary box, everyone started to think that he might just have judged his fractions to perfection. Faithful didn't. He was happy with his position, and merely let out a morsel of rein to match the leader's change of pace. Lima's jockey also sat and waited, happy to allow the field to take a length on his horse, so that he might escape their confines more easily.

Within a hundred yards of making his first move, the jockey on the pacemaker got down behind his horse, and asked him to stretch. Within a few strides, he had his horse at his limit. He was fast and honest, but there was still a long way to go. In behind, the cards were about to be played.

The horse on Lima's outside moved first, and was driven in to making its effort. The response wasn't immediate, and it seemed to take an age for it to increase its advantage over Lima, let alone make any ground on the leader.

Maurice Sheepshanks, in the stands, who, like Min, had accidentally staked more on his horse than he intended, suddenly recalled his initial response to Barrow's plans for the race —that it would turn into a lottery. Crab and Min, a few hundred yards further on from him, were slightly more sanguine, but if a deal was on offer to have their stakes returned, they'd have been second in the queue behind Maurice.

As the horse on Lima's outside moved forward, another came from sitting wide and last, to get into its slipstream. Between the two of them, they gave Lima nowhere to go. If the pacemaker submitted, all would be well, but he kept responding to his rider's urgings. The slow early pace left him with plenty in the tank, and he still travelled well enough to head the arrow of horses, which saw Lima trapped in its middle. Faithful, on the rails, kept the door to his patch locked. There'd be no one to challenge him for that rail pitch today, he knew that, but just in case any of them had forgotten the script, or the unexpected happened, he made sure that there was no daylight between him and the leader.

Favourite backers in the stand prayed for the pacemaker to fall onto the rail, and allow Lima a straight passage through, but Squeezer knew that wasn't going to happen. He leant onto his left rein, and started to ease his horse to the pacemaker's outside. But as he prepared to launch Lima into his challenge, the horse in front of him came alongside the pacemaker and closed what there was of the gap. The outcome of the race balanced on the move that Squeezer, on Lima; and the new horse and jockey, alongside him, did next.

That new arrival on the scene seemed determined to keep Lima boxed in. That wasn't in the plan. Which was the worst outcome now? To finish beaten, hard-held, behind a wall of horses, unable to deliver a challenge; or to force his way out, and make the run he'd been instructed to by Barrow? There was insurance in barging his way out —a poorly pleaded case in front of the stewards would bring about the result that he'd failed to deliver in the race, should it come to that. All these thoughts flashed through his mind in a second. Bang! He squeezed up his horse, threw the reins at him, and forced Lima out sideways. It ended the race for the horse on his outside, but pitched it perfectly for his own, who found his stride, rebalanced, and launched into top gear in one movement.

Squeezer gave him a solid right-hander, and let him go, fast and free, heading for inevitable victory out in the centre of the course. To the watching crowd, the result was now inevitable, and they roared. He'd left it late, but in a matter of strides, he'd made the rest look like they were standing still.

Faithful had been left the perfect passage up the rails, as he'd expected, and as soon as he heard the shouting in behind, got down into his horse, sent him through it, and went flat out for the line. As if coordinated, Min, Crab, and Maurice, bent their heads to the left, to try and find an angle which told them that Astrakhan, going straight up the rail, was on terms with Lima running on a diagonal to their side of the course. It didn't look hopeful, yet, for all of Lima's raw pace, he did seem to be running sideways across the track. A few strides later and suddenly the crowd had the sense that he was going too fast, with no handbrake, and seeming intent on running straight to the stands' rail. He'd pass the post first, sure, but would he still be carrying his jockey when he did? That was the only thought on the minds of those who'd backed him. Squeezer seemed to be struck by the same thought, and fought to straighten him up. Eventually, he persuaded Lima to turn his head away from the stands, and as he did, his horse stopped racing. Whether it was because he'd lost his battle with his jockey; or that he thought he'd beaten all his rivals, and his work was over; was anyone's guess. He had comprehensively trounced the rest of them, that much was true, but, unfortunately for his backers, the winning post was still a hundred yards ahead of him.

It was only when Vino di Vici came up his inside late on, did he realise that he was still in a race, and tried to pick up again. But it was too late and he couldn't do anything to resist the challenge. Astrakhan ran straight and true up the rail, and he'd seen off Lima as planned, but whether he'd done enough to finish in front of the errant Vino di Vici, ridden by the girl apprentice, was another matter. Faithful, once he knew he'd got by Lima, relaxed, as he realised that they'd delivered another job to spec, dropped his hands in the shadow of the post. Twenty seconds later, hearing the announcement of "Photograph, photograph" from the stands, his stomach turned a somersault. Vino di Vici, travelling with such pace at the end of the race as he tried to overhaul his target, Lima, had proved impossible to pull-up for his young jockey, and had taken her on a victory lap. Faithful looked around for her to check her reaction when the photograph announcement was first heard, but she was nowhere in sight. Had she been, he'd have seen an ear to ear beaming smile, celebrating her fifth career victory. She'd got up, and she knew she had. All she had to do now was find a way to persuade her horse to go back to the paddock, then weigh in, before she was declared missing in action.

The sun disappeared behind a cloud, and a chill wind, which had descended the Urals, and rolled across the European plain, picked up speed and venom as it zipped through East Anglia and the Fens, and arrowed its way straight into the grandstand at Leicester racecourse. Every favourite backer; everyone who knew that Lima was a good thing; everyone who was in on the Astrakhan fix, felt it. It went through Crab, then Min; Squeezer, as old, cynical, and familiar with these disasters as he was, felt it too. It went straight through Faithful's belly; it sliced Barrow in two; then stopped to circulate throughout the entire system of Maurice Sheepshanks. "I'm going to be sick," he said to himself, then stood with his hands on the rail to recover, unable to go down and congratulate his horse on his gallant effort, for a moment or two yet.

Min collected Astrakhan and Faithful from the racecourse by the chute, and as soon as he was sure that they were out of earshot of the others, asked, "What happened?"

"No one thought to cover the girl off, on that rag," he said. "She didn't know she was in a jockeys' race."

He said the same thing to Barrow when he dismounted. Squeezer hadn't been quite so generous, "I did my job. If everyone else had done theirs, we'd be alright."

Barrow, not so much red and angry, as purple and apoplectic, disagreed. "You let a girl who could have been settled for fifty quid, come up your inside and nick it? I remember when you used to have wing mirrors."

To Faithful he said, "Who is she, that girl? Find out. And if I discover before you that we've been rolled over, everyone better start running."

"But boss," said Faithful, "She came over the top, someone should have cut her off. I was on the fence, I could only win my race."

"But you didn't. There was a time when you didn't let things like this happen," said Barrow. "You're losing your touch."

As they prepared to leave the winner's enclosure, the bell rang to announce a Steward's Enquiry. They all looked at each other, *have we got out of jail?* But Barrow had it right, "And now one of you is going to get stood down for throwing a race we didn't win. Great job, everybody."

Then Barrow's phone rang, he checked the name, and as soon as he did, looked up to find Min who was occupied with his horse, and couldn't take the call.

"Connie!" he said through a forced smile, "Did you see it?"

Min tried to linger, in the hope of overhearing something useful, and took Astrakhan on another couple of short, warm-down turns of the enclosure.

Barrow had to listen to a barrage of noise and questions as the call began —as hard as he tried, he couldn't interject to take the conversation in his direction. At about the sixth attempt, he said, "Yes, he's got some pure raw talent. We're going to have some fun with him."

He promised to continue the conversation on the drive home, but she wouldn't give up. "He'll have learned an enormous amount from that experience," he told her. "We'll fit him with a pricker bit next time." Then he heard him say, "No, it doesn't mean he's gone rogue. No, if he's good enough to go to stud, it won't make him look ungenuine. One race, maybe we'll even sort him out at home without doing that." Then he trailed off into a series of yesses, edging himself further and further away from anyone who might overhear, as he tried to wind down the call.

Crab picked up Min, as he left the paddock with his horse, "What is the enquiry about?" he wanted to know. "Do you think they fixed a steward as insurance?"

Min laughed. Crab saw every event that ever happened through the prism of insurance. "No. That doesn't happen."

"Why not?" asked Crab. "Everyone's got a price."

"They'd do well to find one corrupt enough to turn that result round," said Min. "It'll be about careless and improper riding."

He was about to take his horse behind the stands to take him through his post-race routine, when Barrow appeared.

"You're going to have to go and see the stewards," he said.

Min was confused, "Me? What do they want me for?"

"This enquiry," said Barrow, making it sound like something or nothing. "You'll just have to confirm the riding instructions."

Min could not readily find a response, "But, I..."

"Don't worry," said Barrow, giving him an amused smile, "I'll take him for you." He took Astrakhan's reins from Min, and moved to the horse's near side, displacing Min, as if pushing him off towards the stewards' rooms.

"What am I going to say?" asked Min.

"A clever lad like you? Go and watch the replay, then just tell them that we told the jockeys to do whatever it was they did."

Min's mouth dried. He looked briefly at Crab for inspiration, but there was none. He watched the whole scene with his mouth open, incredulous to what he was witnessing.

"But what about Lima?" he said.

"What about him?" said Barrow.

"The way he hung across the course."

Barrow looked surprised, and as if they'd started a new conversation said, "He's never done that before, has he?"

He gave Min the nod, to say, *right, go on then, on your way.* "Just tell them you don't know what you're doing, if you get stuck. They can always give me a ring, later."

Once he'd gone, Crab said, "Come on, let's go and have a look at a replay then." Then he added, "Good job, you had that video, and you know the back story, otherwise, you'd be kiboshed."

They watched the rerun of the race together, cobbled together some notes, and Min went off to face his fate.

An hour later, he picked up Crab from the empty grandstands, in the almost empty racecourse, and without speaking gestured for them to head off. Crab could see that his friend was in no mood to talk about his ordeal, just now. He put his hand on his shoulder, and walked along with him in silence. Min had been through a shaming incident that he was still processing, and was in no mood to talk yet. Eventually, still not ready to share the facts of the tribunal directly with Crab, he started talking about the phone call on which he'd eavesdropped between Barrow and Lady Constance.

"It's funny, isn't it? The way they communicate?" said Min.

"What is?" asked Crab.

"I mean, it was totally obvious to anyone who had a brain, that Barrow was making it all up about Lima. When he was talking to her about it, it just all sounded so paper thin —the sort of thing that only an idiot would expect you to believe. And she obviously didn't, and told him so. But if he'd said the same thing to Maurice, or us, we'd just eventually accept what he said, not because we believed him, but because we'd know that he wouldn't give up until we accepted his version of events. But her, she just ploughed on through the embarrassment of it all."

"What do you mean?" said Crab.

"Well, it's never about winning an argument, or persuading someone of a case, is it? It's all just about class, and social standing. She's got the nerve and status to stand up to him. We haven't. That's why Maurice will always be a patsy, and why she never will be. Or if there's the merest hint that she has been abused, it's snuffed out straightaway, and it's a long time 'til he dares do it again.

Crab shrugged, *I suppose so.* He didn't really understand the point Min was making, and took it to be an oblique reference to what had gone on in the enquiry. He was so disconsolate, his friend. As if hope had left his body.

Silence fell again as they walked on into the car park.

When they reached the car, Min put his bag on the roof, and looking over it at Crab said his first words about the humiliation he'd just endured, "They just don't have that capacity for intellectual shame, people like Barrow.

What I've just been through —it's a different sort of ordeal for people like him."

"You're made of better stuff," said Crab. He waited a moment, then added, "Do you think you'll go your separate ways now?"

Min replied, "Crab —me and racing are going to be going our separate ways."

Crab screwed up his face, *what does that mean?*

"There is, as of now, no chance of any sort of career for me as I'd imagined it in horse racing. Perhaps ever," he said. "If I dared to put in an application for a trainer's license within two years of that debacle, it will be stamped *reject* as soon as it's taken from the envelope."

"Oh, I'm sorry Min," said Crab.

They got into the car. "I'll tell you what though," said Min.

"What's that?" asked Crab.

"We were on to their scheme, and we were on the right horse."

"Well, if you're determined to take a positive from it…" said Crab.

"I am," said Min.

"In that case, roll on Plan B, eh? We'll get it all back and more," said Crab.

"I'm already on Plan C," said Min.

-CHAPTER FOUR-

Faithful's fate was confirmed a week or so later. He was to be stood down for a couple of weeks at the end of June, added to which, he was handed down a not insubstantial fine, "What do you think?" he asked Min. "I should appeal, right? Just to help my reputation. I mean I didn't actually cheat —well not in the way they say I did."

They had each metamorphosed into each other's counsellor since *that day*, and were especially so when Barrow was not on the premises. Min was inclined to think that he shouldn't. "Barrow had two horses beaten, when either of them should have won. He won't want it looking into any more than it already has been."

"He could help with the fine though," said Faithful. "We were all carrying out his orders. It someone else's job to take care of that girl, not mine."

"Good luck with that project," said Min.

"He likes you," said Faithful. "Can't you find a way to ask him?"

Min was glad that the boss was away, and said, "I'll do my best for you."

Barrow was in residence at The Cadogan Hotel, Eastbourne. It was his habit to take a few days' break to mark the last days of spring, and begin to sketch out the plan for his summer and autumn campaign, but this time, he had other business to attend to as well. The betting syndicate's rare mistake precipitated a refunding round. He gathered its operatives and managers around him in his suite, and set out the terms on which they'd recoup losses, and take business back to normal.

The operatives were put in funds, and given their instructions. Some would attend the racecourse; others, at various locations close to betting shops, and they were to be ready to work, 'From the first Friday in the month until the Sunday.' They'd be informed of the day with twenty–four hours' notice, and they'd be sent instructions by text, according to their location. The green light for the operatives covering bookmakers shops would be given one hour before the time of the race, and would be followed by a second instruction half an hour later. "It is imperative," said Barrow, "that you submit detailed plans to the email address you'll receive shortly, showing us how you can cover at least six, and ideally up to ten shops, within thirty minutes. Failure to do so, means you'll play no part in the plan." The racecourse activity, would be performed in three passes: one as the horses paraded; the second, as the last horse left the paddock to go to the start, and a third once they'd gone behind and began circling, waiting to be loaded into the stalls.

"As usual, you won't receive the name of the last horse, until you get that final message. You can assume that you'll be backing more than one horse. You may. You may yet back the same horse twice. And no more betting on the Exchanges in running. Your job is to melt into the background. We still haven't found out which of you did that last time, but we will."

He added the usual boilerplate, that their own bets were strictly limited to what they could get on after the syndicate's prices were secured. Every betting slip was to be photographed and sent by text before any money could be collected.

All that said, he dismissed the operatives with their funds, and gathered his intimate backers and owners around him to discuss other details of their plan. One of them owned a building supplies' business, and most of the operatives were his salesmen and women. It was him who told Barrow that he and his fellow investors would require fifty percent return on all funding from now on, before profits were calculated, to reflect the fact that it was a loan, on terms. And, that they would also require the return of the stake lost at Leicester, before any winnings were calculated, on their next venture. Any losses to be carried over. Unless of course, Barrow himself, or other investors he might know, wanted to come in on the funding and share the risk. Barrow didn't. For the time being.

Maurice Sheepshanks was not yet a member of the inner circle, but as his horse was to be part of the plot, he'd be invited to take part in the bet, and, if he played his cards right, perhaps might find his way into being invited into this exclusive club in the coming days and weeks.

That Min's request for leave for the first weekend in June was turned down, came as no surprise. That it was declined because, "I need my best people around me, then," did. Min crossed with Faithful as he left the office, smiling at him in response to his wink.

When they next talked, Faithful confirmed his suspicions, "I'm sorry," said Min, "I probably mucked that up for you, getting him in a bad mood before you went in."

"It wouldn't have made any difference," Faithful said. Barrow, according to his version of events, had been determined to draw a line under their spat with a decisive statement of their master-servant relationship. To his request that the fine be split, Barrow had replied that it would 'Do him good,' on the basis that he'd be watchful of falling foul of the stewards in the future. Barrow's had been the last word in their meeting: "Just do your job next time, and we'll have a think about renewing your contract.

"I suppose it means that there will be a next time, at least," said Faithful. Min was sure of that. But whether it would involve Faithful, he was less confident.

Besides, he had his own problems to deal with. That night he picked up the phone to Crab. On reflection, he shouldn't have opened with, "Do you want the good news or the bad?" It had made too light of an expensive write-off that was in large part down to him. Paris was now off, and the costs so far incurred, were to be thrown away. He would have been reluctant to go anyway, given the losses suffered at Leicester, but Barrow's declining his request for leave, helped to make that decision for him; and he had raised that possibility with Crab when the idea of the trip had been first mooted. By that token, Crab's impetuosity meant that he shared some of the responsibility too. He should have presented it all like that, instead of owning it with a weak joke.

"This is going to be a hard deal to broker at home. We're going to have to come up with a convincing alternative," he said. "How's Jane taken it?"

A cold lead weight dropped to the pit of Min's stomach.

He was going to talk to her next, once the alternatives had been kicked around with Crab. Eventually, they settled on a box at Epsom, with Min, as a special punishment for his having cried-off, challenged to come up with three Michelin stars over the course of the weekend. "All in one restaurant; a two and a one; or in three individuals," Crab had stipulated. And his final term: that it must all take place within striking distance of an airport, just in case they managed a good day at the races between them. "All winnings to be for communal use," he added.

All that settled, their conversation moved on to more specific matters. "So," said Crab. "You've blown my money on Paris and Astrakhan, it's time for the good news, isn't it?"

It wasn't just because he was desperate to leave the bad news behind; he had been bursting to tell Crab what he knew about Lima, and what Faithful had so far shared with him about the horse. "Faithful rides him every day now," he told him. "And in their first proper piece of work since the race, as he came off the gallop he said to me, out of earshot of the boss, 'Squeezer must be some jockey to have got beat on this thing.' He's the best horse in the yard," he added.

"Mmmh," Crab was reluctant to disagree with Min directly, "Are you sure, you're sure? Think of that scene at Leicester, Min. It looked like amateur hour. And the horse! If ever there was a horse that merited a squiggle by its name, it was Lima."

Min would not have it. He saw the horse every day. He heard Faithful's little throwaway comments about him. For him, that Lima had been beaten at all showed the genius of the operation. "Imagine if that girl hadn't got the chance ride, you'd have been praising Barrow and his syndicate now for their cold native cunning. And the execution! Your word Crab, their brilliant execution of the coup."

"That's my point," said Crab. "They didn't. Something unexpected happened, and they weren't ready for it. They even lost their insurance bet. That's not how it's supposed to work."

They argued the point back and forth. Min now knew how long these jockeys' races had been a feature of

UK racing. He knew how seldom they failed. Crab was at arm's length from all that. He didn't know, as Min now did, the extent to which this way of doing things was woven into the fabric of routine racing round the gaffs, and the old country tracks; how it turned barely break-even prize money, into opportunities for profits for journeymen jockeys and bottom of the rung owners. And how Barrow had learnt his trade there, and had the means, owners, and audacity to apply it at a higher level of racing too.

"Come on up," said Min.

"What?"

"Come up and see it with your own eyes. Listen to what the jockey says when Barrow's not there. Judge for yourself. I'll tell him you're a prospective owner."

"Do you think I'm made of holidays?" Crab asked.

"That's a point," said Min. "Maybe we can check out a restaurant for your stag weekend in the evening?"

"Dear me. You're such an expensive indulgence," said Crab.

"I'll tell the boss, that I'll refer to Lima by a different name in your presence so that he'll let you see him work. As soon as I know the day, I'll text you," said Min.

"Won't he remember me from Leicester?" asked Crab, "I am a tall poppy, you know."

"But barely visible when seen through red mist," said Min. "And so what? I know you from my old job.

He'll say yes, if he thinks you're worth a fortune —just bring the full City regalia with you."

"For you Min, I might even slip on a pair of penny loafers."

Min put down his phone, then turned his attention to Jane. It had been a hard enough sell to persuade her to blow their entire holiday budget on forty-eight hours of hedonism in Paris. It was going to be tougher still to tell her that a similar sum was to be spent on a private box at the races, for a day on which he would be required to work. So, he decided not to. Nor did he tell her, that he would be borrowing from reserves to find the stake for Plan B, and to settle the debts that had gone west on Plan A.

With about three weeks to go to the race, Crab arrived at Barrow's yard. It sat behind the County Stud, occupying the corner plot between the two London Roads, at a remove from the main action of the town where everyone else had their yards.

"So, is he for sale?" asked Crab, as Lima breezed past his work companion, in the last piece of work that morning.

"Saturn? No, he's spoken for, I'm afraid," said Barrow laughing. "You've got to have a few goes at horseracing before you land on one like him. We've got plenty of nice horses, though, and they all look like he did about a year or so ago. That colt you saw at first lot's one of them, he's probably the best investment, but there's only half of him left. And there's two fillies, I know you liked them, but like I said, they're more for next year now. Let Min show you the rest, then come back and see me."

He nodded his goodbyes, then turned to go and meet Lima from the gallop. As he did, the horse was already within twenty–five yards of them. "That was quick," he said, reacting as if there had been a conspiracy to sneak up on him quickly, and unseen.

"Couldn't put out a candle, boss," said Faithful. Barrow changed direction again to follow the horse in, nodded goodbye once more to Crab as he passed him again, then went back to his conversation with Faithful.

"Come on," said Min, "I'll show you those other horses."

Crab smiled and mouthed, "Sociopath," giving Min a thumbs-up.

Beyond their earshot, Faithful, in return for dropping his request for Barrow's assistance in his pursuit of justice with the stewards, tried to turn it into a quid pro quo. He pitched his case to ride Lima, telling Barrow that he was finally getting into the horse's head, and "Could turn him into a machine."

But Barrow was not prepared to negotiate his plans. "Yes, you're the stable jockey. That's your job," he said.

Faithful had started to say, "He's getting to trust me," but Barrow, not listening, still locked into his train of thought, continued, talking over him, "With you up, it looks like we believe that Astrakhan's our best horse, and was an unlucky loser, last time" he said. "If you ride this lad," and he slapped Lima behind the saddle, "it's as good as telling everyone what only we know."

When Faithful persisted with his point, Barrow lost his patience, and ended all further talk on the subject by saying, "Why don't you just stick to coming second? You're good at that."

Min and Crab were finishing their tour of the small, second yard, as Barrow left for lunch, "Still here?" he called, and went to say a formal, final, goodbye to Crab. "I really think the value's in the colt," he said. "Unless you fancy taking a pop at the yearling sales? They'll come round soon enough. Ask Min about them."

"Maybe he's just an arsehole," said Crab, as Barrow disappeared from view. "And what's that hair all about? If he wasn't receding at the temples, he'd have a bob. He's got a flair for insurance though —see the way he dropped the yearling sales in, just in case I don't like anything he's got for sale?" He and Min walked on, out of the yard, cutting the corner of the main yard into the car park, and took their conversation back to the more pressing matter of Lima and his next race, as they did.

"I'm not comfortable about going all-in on a horse with foibles," said Crab.

"Characteristics," Min corrected him. "Don't forget what Faithful said about Leicester —that it was a work of genius to be able to disguise his talents so well. Hey, here he is."

Faithful swerved on the route to his car. "No good boys, he won't let me have the ride on Lima, at any price," and he told them about his conversation with Barrow. "It was important to be seen to be trying, though," glancing briefly at Min as he said it.

"I suppose they had so much money on Astrakhan last time," said Crab, "that most people will think he's the better horse —and Barrow wants to make everything keep pointing that way."

Faithful nodded to concede a fair point, but wasn't convinced. "I could have that Lima bulletproof, if he'd let me," he said. "And the important thing is to win the race next time. No mistakes."

"How good might he be?" asked Crab.

Faithful laughed. The question was so far beyond the protocol of racing stable etiquette, it was ridiculous. He knew Min's pal was safe, but keeping secrets and obfuscating facts was deeply ingrained in his system, and it just didn't come naturally to him to speak in that way to strangers. He noticed Min tip his head to assure him that Crab really was one of them, and so eventually, after a couple of false starts, he managed to say, "He works like a hundred and five, hundred and ten, horse."

Min raised his eyes at Crab, who asked, "What is he now?"

"Seventy–two," said Min. He turned to Faithful to prevent Crab from developing the conversation with him any further, and said, "Are you saying he's getting Squeezer in every morning, to ride him?"

"Oh no. He won't have him in here for a while. Not after stitching him at Leicester last time."
Min shot him a puzzled look. "You make it sound like he's scared of him."

"Of Squeezer? No, don't be daft. But he's wary of some of his followers. He won't want any of them getting too close to things round here 'til it's all long forgotten about," said Faithful. "Have you not noticed the way he looks over his shoulder every ten paces? No, I'll still be doing all the hard work, don't worry about that."

He set off without another word, then called out, "See you later, Min," then sent a, "Nice to meet you," towards Crab, as he walked his bow-legged walk to his car.

"You've got a bitch-mate at last," said Crab, slapping Min on the shoulder. "Things are looking up."

They strolled over to Crab's car.

"Who would you prefer to see ride Lima at Epsom?" he asked, and Min, without hesitation, replied, "Him," and pointed in the direction Faithful had left. Crab raised his palms as if to say, *do you see my point?* to which Min replied, "That is why *we*," and he stressed the *we*, "must plan this properly. Better even than Barrow could manage."

"Properly?" said Crab. "Are you sure you're not better suited to a life in the City?"

"No! Maybe. Why?" asked Min.

"Because you make your begging sound like you're doing me a favour," said Crab, and he stressed the *me*.

Min smiled.

"Let's go to that cubby hole of yours up the High Street, and plan our futures," said Crab.

"There's nothing I'd like better," said Min.

-CHAPTER FIVE-

Barrow fielded his A—team for the race. Min was
to be deployed as an actual assistant for once, rather than a
substitute lad. That meant that he'd be on hand to do
Barrow's bidding as events unfolded. He was to leg up
Astrakhan; Barrow, Lima.

He first dropped off Jane at the box they'd hired
for the afternoon. It was to be a surprise —Min was still
trying to make up lost ground from the cancelled Paris
trip, but it didn't go down that way. Jane was confused,
and not a little bit annoyed to find herself in this odd place
on a Friday afternoon. A waiter hovered, and there was an
open buffet lunch set out at the back of the box.
Champagne chilled in the funny little room with a balcony,
that was decorated to resemble something between a
private room in a hospital and a mid-range apart-hotel.
Crab came in from the balcony, and made a better
job of making her feel that she was on a day out. He
poured her a glass of champagne without asking what she
wanted to drink, then ushered her out to meet his seldom-
seen fiancé, Eleanor.
In truth, Crab was her host. He'd covered the
costs of the box, and he'd be buying dinner if their plan
failed to come to fruition. He'd been generous in the

settlement of the Leicester losses with Min too, and had funded the lion's share of what was to be their stake today. In that last act, he took Min's debt to him from one that needed to be repaid in instalments over the course of a year, to one in which he would be demoted behind Min's mortgage provider, bank, and other sundry creditors in the queue for repayment.

A pair from the three Donahue sisters smiled a quick hello to her, as they headed into the box to meet Min. There was an older male out there too. Crab introduced him, but in the swirling confusion of activity and unfamiliar names and faces, she lost her concentration and missed his name. The question, "I'm sorry who is he, again?" began to form on her lips, but she didn't go through with it

The two sisters walked directly towards Min. Without uttering a word, they each offered him a hand in a sombre greeting, as if they were all accomplices about to go before the judge. Min smiled a thanks, declined a drink from the waiter, then tried to slip out, unnoticed by Jane, as he went to work. Crab caught him doing it out of the corner of his eye, as the sisters returned. "Be careful out there!" he called after him.

It was meant as a joke, but it only served to heighten Jane's anxiety and discomfort.

The man called, "I'd better get going too," and waved a goodbye to Crab.

"Thank you, Michael," he called back. "See you later." Then he turned his attentions back to Jane, and said, "Don't fret, Janey, he'll be back in a minute." Jane's weak smile seemed to say, *I no longer believe anything either of you say.* She took a sip from her drink, then asked Crab if she was allowed to smoke on the balcony. He shrugged.

"What did that mean, *be careful?*" she asked, drawing deeply on her cigarette.

Crab gestured with his hand to the crowds below, "Here be dragons," he said, and left it at that.

Lady Constance, unlike Faithful, did not have a clock built into her system. Her lunches were unmeritedly fabled. Their excesses better explained by the fact that she could not distinguish between dinnertime and lunch. The few who could speak with hard-earned experience of such things, included breakfast in that too. She seldom slept during the night, preferring to watch replays of her horses over and over, so that she was better placed to advise how they might improve next time. And during the day, she was often indisposed to the trainers, agents, jockeys and all their assistants who reluctantly returned her calls. Though, there were cross-over periods at the start and end of normal working days, when a lot of time was spent in a telephone conversation for anyone unfortunate enough to find themselves in a commercial relationship with her.

Faithful touched the peak of his cap as she came to join their circle. Inscrutable behind her bug-eye sunglasses, and upturned collar on the scarlet cashmere coat which reached the calves of her small round frame, his cocky and vicious demeanour, was no match for her cold disdain.

The small circle comprised Min, who was to leg him up on Astrakhan, Maurice Sheepshanks, and two other men resembling close protection officers who seemed neither to be in it, nor elsewhere. Min and Maurice, who had not learnt the protocol with which to address her ladyship, each nodded a greeting in turn, and hoped that no more would be said. It wasn't. Lady Constance offered them a begrudging movement of her lips, which on any other face, would not have been called a smile.

At least a minute of awkward silence had been endured, when Barrow arrived, trying not to let it show that he had spent the last two hours in Lady Constance's company.

"All well?" he asked, clapping his hands, trying to insinuate the idea that horse racing was a great theatre of fun for everyone lucky enough to be associated with it. "Well let's get this race won with one of ours, eh?" he threw into the silence.

Squeezer joined the group, tipped his cap to Lady Constance, sparing everyone from hearing what she was about to say, which he followed with a cursory, unmeant, handshake to Min and Maurice. He then withdrew to the edge of the circle to stand in self-contained insolence, until the time came to get on his horse.

A couple of Barrow's syndicate arrived shortly behind Squeezer, which prompted Barrow into escorting Lady Constance into her own space. He braved the dense fug of Dubonnet infused Chanel No. 5 mixed with what someone had once described as *that old-lady smell*, suggesting to her that she come to have a look at her horse parading. "We've turned him inside out since Leicester," he said.

Lady Constance was his special client, and he did not lightly expose her to others. Particularly soulless grifters like Squeezer, who would have any number of contacts in his circle who'd happily bend to her ladyship's whims. She had been his greatest training feat. Her prompt settlement of invoices provided the cashflow on which his business was run. And, in addition to all that, their discussions at lunch had not yet been concluded, and he definitely did not want any of his underlings to witness his owner's instinct for searing honesty which he bore as the cost of all the other benefits she brought.

Min and Maurice, by whom they passed on their way out of the circle, overheard the first part of that conversation. Something about, "Your boy didn't say that when he worked before Leicester. The opposite in fact." The boy in question, Min, was only pleased that he didn't have to listen to Barrow's reply as their voices trailed away —or any of the conversation that followed, for that matter, as Barrow frequently cast his gaze sideways towards Min and the others, as each of them was traduced in turn by his Connie. They couldn't be overheard, but the silent gathering knew that none of them were coming out of it well. But it was the occasional guffaw from Barrow that rankled with them most. Particularly Maurice, who'd expected something closer to a thanks for running his horse, given that it was the quid pro quo in a deal in which the quo had not happened.

The bell rang, and Barrow returned. "Let's go to it," he said to no one in particular. It was such an out of character statement, a collective wince went round the little circle.

One of the unnamed men took a step further back, and took out his phone, as Min gestured to Faithful to slip away quietly with him. They went together to the quiet bottom corner of the paddock, and waited for Astrakhan to come round to them, rather than seek out the horse. Neither man spoke.

He legged up Faithful into the saddle, then trotted round to the offside of the horse to walk along with him. "Everything OK?" he asked, as they reached the chute.

Faithful looked dead ahead into the distance, and said, "Never better." A few strides later, he asked, "Is he just backing Lima? The little man."

It took a moment to register that he meant Maurice.

"I don't know. I imagine so." Min was taken unawares by the question, and didn't immediately get Faithful's point. The jockey said no more. Content to leave his words with Min to mull over in his own time.

They didn't speak another word. Min walked with Astrakhan to within ten yards of the racecourse, and watched him spin off to the start. He gave the paddock sheet to his lass, and walked back down the chute, alone, ordering his thoughts in readiness for what was to come.

After a while, he realised that he was walking in step with Vino di Vici's trainer, Gary Boswell. He didn't have a horse in the race, and Min suddenly realised he'd been sought out.

"What are you up to this time, then?" asked Boswell.

"Same old," said Min. He was the sort of trainer he'd avoid, even if he were not on duty for Barrow. He looked about him to see if Barrow was anywhere nearby.

"I hope not," said Boswell laughing, "It nearly got you in a lot of trouble, last time."

Min ignored him.

"Would have, it hadn't had been for me."

Min tried to drag out the silence 'til they reached the paddock, when he could peel off and wave goodbye, but Boswell didn't seem disposed to go away. And the paddock was a step away yet. "What hadn't?"

"Not dropping you in it, when you were up to no good," he said. He kept slowing in his stride, trying to draw Min into stopping so that they could have a proper chat, but Min would not play ball.

"You won the race, didn't you? Weren't you happy with that?" Min said, irked now that he wouldn't let it go. Boswell lingered a couple of strides behind him still.

"No, as it goes, I wasn't," said Boswell. "I was warned off having a bet. I was only asking if your lot fancied either of yours, so I'd know how much to have on, then I just got told to do one, and stay away from the ring by one of those bruisers that hangs around with him."

Min said nothing. But suddenly he liked the way the conversation was going.

"Them who are here again today," Boswell added.

Min had reached the part of the chute where it turned back to the paddock, and saw that Boswell had stopped close to the place where they untack the beaten horses after the race —empty now of people and horses before the race began. Min looked about him, then took a couple of paces back towards Boswell.

"I won't spoil nowt, for you. I only want to make up for last time," said Boswell.

"Look, I'm busy, and I haven't got time for this," said Min, publicly, he hoped. Then he leaned in closer to Boswell, as if to say the harsher words that he did not want to be overheard, and said, "Lima cannot be beat."

Boswell considered the offer for a moment. "No. Too easy. I'm not buying."

Min shrugged, "Barrow would put you away — he'd do it to his best friend. But he wouldn't invite Lady

Constance to the races to watch her horse, then do it to her. She's too important to him." He indicated Barrow on the far steps, taking his leave of Lady Constance.

Boswell's sly grin broadened into a real one.

"Don't go gangbusters on it and ruin their price," he added. "Not for my sake —for your own." He set off, then stopped, and came back. "That's the best tip you'll ever get, by the way. Watch your step, 'cos someone else will be watching you."

As Min re-entered the paddock, Barrow beckoned him. He took him to the same quiet corner in which Min had legged up Faithful. It was empty now, on both sides of the rail. Barrow pulled open Min's jacket, put a package into its inside breast pocket, and said "Spread that about on Lima. But not a penny on, 'til they've gone behind."

Min nodded his head in compliance, as he froze inside.

In the faraway days of the clubs and gaming rooms of St. James, where horseracing first established its origins, men would stake their reputation and their family's heritage on the outcome of a match between their horse and another man's. Here, today, losing might not wipe either of them out, but the journey back from being on the wrong horse, would be hard, long, and slow. And just like they were in those olden times, neither Min nor Barrow, contemplated losing as a likely option.

He waited until Barrow was out of sight then called Crab, "Last min_te hitch," he said, and relayed the news of the unexpected snag to their finely tuned plan.

In the background Min could hear Jane say, "What is it? What's happened now?"

"I'll call you back," said Crab.

Crab put his finger to his lips to tell Jane to give him a moment alone with his thoughts. He unpacked his and Min's laptops, and set them up on the table which contained the buffet, then logged them both into a betting exchange app. He turned his attention back to Jane, and charged her with keeping an eye on them until they returned, which he assured her, would be very soon. He spent another moment telling her that all would be well, then called Min back to say that he'd be with him in a moment to lend a hand with his task, and arranged a meeting spot.

Crab was sitting at the circular bench, in the courtyard by the main grandstand, when Min arrived breathless from the paddock, each of them at pains to disguise from the other the rate at which their hearts were racing. They had planned to be back in their box together by now, all preparations set before the final execution, yet here they were, with unforeseen tasks still to be dealt with, as the seconds ticked down to post time.

The last horse had gone to the start, where the others circled in front of the stalls. Soon they'd be taken behind.

"As I see it, we have three choices," said, Crab, "all of which will get you the sack. I know that's of no concern to you, but whether any other consequences flow from that..." and he grimaced.

"Things are improving," thought Min. He thought there'd been just two.

Crab continued, "If we put Barrow's bet on, as instructed, we lose our chance of a decent insurance bet ourselves. And maybe, we run out of time to do what we came here to do. So that's out. If we put his on now, it will ruin his price but it will help ours. That's an option. And there might be scope to nick a bit of that for ourselves if we get some tasty prices."

"That's what we're doing," said Min. He told him how he'd just sent Boswell off to back Lima too. "Let's turn this negative into a positive, and back Lima off the boards."

They set off at a jog, a jogging-shuffle in Crab's case.

"By the way, what was the third option?" asked Min, as Crab stopped to lean on a wastebin, to catch his breath.

"Oh," said Crab, sheepishly, "that? I was going to say that we could take the nuclear option, and add Barrow's stake to our own."

Min stared at him in disbelief, "You. A man of insurance! Go and wash your mouth out with soap," he said.

"I'm sorry," said Crab. "The excitement must be getting to me. Promise you'll never tell anyone I said that."

The race day crowd around them busied themselves for the race. A wave of them passed through, returning from the paddock, heading towards the Tote windows, and bookmakers pitches. All of them, from the regulars to the day trippers; from the people who devoted too much of their lives to the conundrum of horse racing, and who longed to make a living from it, to the professionals who did; from the people who thought that it was a real live lottery played out in front of their eyes, to those who could explain it all through the science of breeding; they all anticipated a fair contest, in which the best, and sometimes luckiest, horse on the day prevailed. They did not understand that they were participating in an event, the outcome of which was already known, to but a few of their fellow racegoers.

Barrow, divested of Lady Constance settled himself in front of the screen in the main paddock, to watch. His operatives stood in readiness at the edge of the ring. Squeezer's followers in different parts of the country had already started to make their play. Maurice Sheepshanks, from his eerie high up in the stands convinced himself that he was spying on it all, as suddenly, as if to confirm all his worst suspicions, Min came into range of his binoculars.

He shuffled sideways down the steep concrete steps and made his way to the back rank of bookmaker's pitches to intercept Min and Crab in their nefarious activities.

"What's going on?" he asked.

The racecourse announcer cut through the noise, "They're going behind."

"They're going behind," said Min.

Maurice gave him a sarcastic smile.

"Nothing," said Min.

"It doesn't look like nothing," said Maurice. "The signal's not been given yet. Look!" and he pointed aimlessly towards the lower steps of the stand, where he thought he'd spotted some people who looked like they might be Barrow's operatives.

"We're backing the wrong one, to help the price," Min lied.

"What? My horse?" said Maurice, "but that's drifting. Look." This time he pointed towards the bookmakers' boards.

Beads of sweat had formed on Min's forehead. He had neither the time nor the energy to find a way out of the argument with Maurice, so he simply said, "You should too."

"What?" said Maurice.

"How would you feel if your horse won, and you didn't even have a little insurance on him?"

Maurice was confused, from where he quickly progressed to enraged. All of his assumptions, misapprehensions, and conspiracy theories as to what really went on with these people, were being confirmed in front of his eyes; all his doubts and disappointments, suddenly finding the outlet they'd so long sought.

"You know the trouble with you lot, don't you?" he said, reddening, his breathing becoming faster and shallower. "You couldn't lie straight in bed. None of you."

He left them with his words, then retired to the low steps of the grandstand to consider his options.

"Well, you can't say I didn't try," said Min.

They arrived back in their box a couple of minutes later, their clothes stuck to them by the perspiration of their efforts. Immediately Jane approached them, less enjoying a day out at the races, more, the partner of someone she imagined to be in the course of being chased down by criminals. Or worse, the police.

"A minute, please," he begged of her, accepting his laptop from Crab. He perched it on his knee, refusing drinks, and napkin to mop his sweating face, and went to his work in parallel with Crab. They immediately saw by how much Lima's price had collapsed, and looked up at each other to exchange a wry grin. Jane paced, unable to shake off her nerves. Everyone else in the box maintained a respectful silence for the work now underway.

With all the flourish of a concert pianist, Crab banged the enter key with his little finger to conclude his transaction, then slapped down the lid of his laptop with his other hand.

"What's happened now?" asked Jane. "Someone, one of you, please explain to me, what's going on. Our trip to Paris is cancelled, yet you spend the same money on a box at the races. Then we don't see you all day, while you work, and you, well both of you, are up to something that's extremely frightening to observe. You're both so clever, yet you're so easily drawn into this ridiculous gambling underworld. You never win you know. In the end. You never win. It's all fixed.

"You're absolutely right, Jane," said Crab. "And now, the fix is in."

The crowd outside suddenly hushed to tune into the familiar rhythmical monotone burr that conveyed the early stages of the racecourse commentary; and as the quiet fell, everyone's attention in the box turned to the TV screens dotted all around it.

Two horses immediately went to the front, and shared pacemaking duties. Between them, they set a good swinging gallop, and the remaining eight runners behind them, were free to choose their own place in the wide-open spaces of Epsom. As they began to swing left-handed for the first time the two pacemakers were still to give their intentions away.

Lima was anchored plum last, all options open. Astrakhan to the far side of the trailing pack was mid-division, his jockey set on making the far rail his, if the field headed that way. The pacemakers went on unchallenged, and as they reached the top of the descent, finally committed to the stand's rail. Faithful rushed up his horse to take closer orders, and as he did, Barrow, watching the big screen in the paddock turned to Maurice, who'd crept alongside him, and said, "Maybe there's not enough pace on?" Squeezer, sat last still, seemed unconcerned. He ignored Faithful's move, and kept his horse to the far side of the chasing peloton.

Astrakhan continued to make steady progress on the two leaders. He moved to sit on their tails as the grandstands came close, allowing nothing to slip between him and them, in the dash for the line. As they continued downhill, the pacemaker furthest from him, changed his legs, unbalanced for a stride or two, and rolled off his line. Instinctively, the other pacemaker, went slightly left with him, and in doing so, left a clear gap to the rail. Faithful pushed his horse into it, switched his stick to his left hand, and gave Astrakhan a kick in the belly to maintain his momentum as he reached the bottom of the hill.

In behind, Squeezer changed his hands, and without another horse in his lane, passed the labouring field in a matter of strides. As he hit the rising ground, only the pacemaker and Astrakhan to his right, were still in front of him. He too drew his stick to his left hand, but before he so much as thought of giving his horse a flick behind the saddle, Lima changed his legs, and flew, straight as a gun barrel, ready for a battle with the leaders.

Faithful knew he was coming, and as the descent began to level out, he sat for a couple of strides, rebalanced his horse, and declined the dogfight. In that fleeting moment, Lima found himself two lengths in front, and going away.

Only Astrakhan was capable of keeping up the pursuit, running on doggedly against the rail, with his jockey throwing everything he had at his horse. It seemed a lost cause, but he kept on keeping on, when Squeezer and Lima knew that the race was theirs. But Faithful never gave up, and kept after his horse, head down, driving for all he was worth. And, plucky little Astrakhan responded to his urgings, giving all he had in pursuit of his stablemate. There was no such thing as a lost cause in Faithful's book, and as experience went, he had as much as anyone in the race. He dared a glance up, and saw his rival begin to shorten his stride. Lima had started to hang left down the camber, as he began to pull himself up. Everything went into slow motion as the unrelenting uphill finish went into its last fifty gruelling yards. Then, as the mown line came into view, Astrakhan was in the lead, and at the line, he was going away from the horse in second.

Not so much a chill wind, as a tremor from the very bowels of the earth, rumbled through the paddock. Barrow remained in the position from where he'd watched the race, dead still in quiet contemplation, as it rippled through his body. Maurice Sheepshanks decided in that moment that he could stop a runaway train with his curse, and vowed to give up horse racing and gambling for the rest of his life.

Everyone in Barrow's circle wore the deep shock of what they'd just witnessed on their faces. The good thing turned over! The racing certainty that was, yet wasn't. Who had stitched up who? They exchanged glances around their gang to look at the reaction in their fellow rogues, and saw their own reflected back. A deep sense of shock and betrayal ran through everyone in the syndicate, it's funders, it's operatives, the wider camp that helped make it all happen; all bar Faithful, who had spent most of the last month turning Lima's quirks into reliable character traits.

Never had the syndicate suffered two consecutive losers. It would need re-building from scratch. Barrow would be in for a share of that, besides his part in the loans gone west.

"Well, I'd better at least see them in," Crab said to Jane. "Are you coming?"

"Where's Min?' she asked, suddenly as terrified as she'd been all day.

Min had slipped out quietly as soon as he saw Lima start to pull himself up. He'd gone to walk in with the winner, as he'd be expected to do.

Crab and Jane hit the steps of the paddock, just as Min came in with Faithful and Astrakhan to the winner's spot.

"Did he just wink at you?" asked Jane. "It was, it was a wink. I saw it."

Crab shrugged, *it might have been.*

"So," she said, "does that mean it's good news, or bad?"

Crab didn't answer. Instead, he beckoned her down a couple of steps, to get closer to the action, so that they might catch some of what was said as they watched the unfolding events.

To the disinterested observer, and the TV cameras, Barrow's first instinct, to commiserate with the connections of the horse that had finished second, marked him out as the man of good grace and exquisite manners that they knew him to be. In truth, he lacked the composure to deal with the winner. He hadn't yet put together his case to prosecute that matter. He'd have to, and he would have to do it quickly if he was to save the day: They were overwhelming, the consequences of losing: money; debts; followers; backers; his principal owner. Anyone of those things, if not dealt with properly could put a hole in his business from which it might not recover, but without her, it just wasn't viable. And new Lady Constance's didn't come along as often as they once did.

He attempted to keep his back to the crowd and the cameras, as he tried to plead his mitigation to her, knowing that as soon as he turned round to face the public, he'd need to change his expression from shock and dread, into one of tolerable contentment at the outcome. But Constance made that task all the more difficult by edging away from him each time he brought himself within whispering distance.

He wasn't going to win her over, there and then, but until he'd established a foothold in his negotiations with her, the other connections would have to present the team's happy smiling faces to the outside world. Min and Faithful, did not exactly embrace all that; and Maurice Sheepshanks, the lucky owner, did not display any of the joy of having a winner at all. He remained stock still between both camps, rooted in temporary paralysis; everything that went with the aftermath of a race run, swirling around him, in blurred slow motion. He felt he should move, but something prevented him from finding the impetus to go to his left or his right. Both seemed wrong simultaneously: to attend the post mortem of the horse he'd backed; or to congratulate his own, which had won the race. So, he remained standing, immobile, not knowing whether to laugh or cry, until eventually, as his senses began to return, he chose the latter.

Barrow gave up on his humiliating pursual of Lady Constance having made no significant headway, and turned his attention to Squeezer. As he came within talking distance, Squeezer said, "He just stopped on me, boss. He's a wrong 'un."

Barrow replied, "That's why I told you to produce him on the line. It's why we put that other horse in the race, to give you the pace and the target to run at. Who's organised this? Your backers? Is this their revenge for what happened at Leicester?"

Squeezer had never been what you'd call a conversationalist, but he was lost for words now. He'd been on the best horse in the race, he knew the money was down, and all he'd wanted to do, was to make sure. He knew that the horse wouldn't stop. He'd ridden him at Leicester and it was him that had stopped the horse, not the other way about. Besides which, there hadn't been another horse to run at.

"If anyone was angry after Leicester, they'll be angrier now," was the best way Squeezer could think of putting it.

Barrow, went ashen, and instinctively looked for dangers close by.

"Someone's fixed him, guvnor. It wasn't me, I was just trying to win the race, clear."

"You've forgotten how to sit and wait on a horse!" said Barrow. He almost shouted, "Do you think I'm as thick as you?" If anyone was in the mood for a fight with him, he was ready to give them one back. He left Squeezer, to see the winners.

"Go and talk to Constance, please Min," he said. "See if you can talk some sense into her."

"The woman who calls me boy, and doesn't trust a word I say?" he asked.

"Just go and do what you can," said Barrow.

He took the bucket from which Astrakhan had been drinking, and poured it carefully over his back. Then he walked with the empty bucket to place it with the others, lined against the short rail that enclosed the area from the rest of the paddock. From there, he went unswervingly towards Lady Constance ignoring her attempts to warn him off. He said, "Hard luck," as unsympathetically as he could manage, then stood close by her, for the simple purpose of getting on her nerves, while Barrow did whatever it was, he wanted to do.

"I'm going to pull some strings and get an enquiry announced. I'll need you to say that you barged your way through," Barrow told Faithful.

Faithful laughed. "The trouble with that is, I didn't" He turned away from Barrow as if he was going to weigh-in, then stopped to complete the thought. "Added to which, the stewards already think I'm a cheat, or ride for one."

Astrakhan's lass struggled alone to put the winner's cooler sheet, on her horse, and she beckoned Min to come back and help her. Faithful grabbed a rein to help her out.

Barrow swallowed deeply, his disquiet etched into his face, "Look, Faithful, we need this. The yard, the horses, our jobs —they're in the balance. You've got to take one for the team here."

"What exactly are you asking me to do?" asked Faithful.

Barrow glanced down at his saddle and weight cloth which Faithful clutched under his arm, then came in closer.

"Weigh in light," he said in an urgent whisper, then gave Faithful a dead-eyed look, to tell him it was an instruction, not a request.

Min arrived and took the reins from him, "She said she'll call you at home as usual," he lied, vaguely turning his head in Barrow's direction, unconcerned whether he heard what he said, or not. Faithful tried to catch his eye, but Min missed the gesture.

He'd long anticipated this moment, Faithful, but now it was here, it was anything but how he'd imagined it. He'd expected Barrow to have rumbled them already, and all his preparations had been made for that outcome. Events had now taken a very different, and much more sinister course. No longer could he deliver his prepared response: to repeat Barrow's own line back to him, that "You must be losing your touch."

To help Faithful in his deliberations, Barrow, noting his hesitance, added, "Otherwise, I'm going to have to report you both for not riding to instructions." Faithful shook his head at him, as he tried to process the thousand different thoughts into the one that mattered. Seconds hung like hours, as he fought to find the right words. He looked up to Min for assistance, but couldn't locate him.

Finally, he came in close to Barrow and said, "Do your worst," as a suited figure approached them from behind. It was as if he'd always been there, observing, but had only become apparent as Astrakhan's lass walked him on a wider arc, no longer blocking the view of the other people milling around them. Barrow sensed his presence, thinking him to be one of the lackeys from racecourse administration, come to hurry them along into their prize giving positions, or invite them up to watch a rerun of the race over a glass of champagne.

The man, Sir Michael, whispered quietly over the shoulders of their conspiratorial huddle, that the "Horses away," instruction had been given already, and they were making everyone late.

"Yes, yes, we're doing it," said Barrow, impatiently waving him away, without turning to look at him.

"So, you'd better get yourself weighed-in," the man said to Faithful.

They both turned to see the imposing figure of Sir Michael, who returned Faithful's fearful gaze with a raised eyebrow. Faithful's face softened into a smile, and he went to do as he was instructed. To Barrow, Sir Michael said, "Congratulations. But I think you'd be better employed getting your boys weighed in before the runner up beats you to it with a complaint. Is this the winning owner, over here?" and he pointed with his thumb towards Maurice Sheepshanks, who stood like a pillar of salt, still, save for the tear which ran from his good eye.

"This is too weird for words," said Jane. "What's going on?"

Crab, exhaled, and readied himself to speak to her.

"I don't like that Min works with this lot. It feels dangerous, threatening, somehow." She was looking at the figures just beyond the enclosure who had kept Barrow, Min, and Faithful under scrutiny the entire time, they were there.

"I don't think he is going to be working for them for much longer," said Crab. He meant it as a placatory statement, to begin his conversation with her, but it produced the opposite reaction from the one he'd hoped for in Jane.

Jane sucked in her breath and tried to keep her thoughts to herself, but failed. "I knew it, I knew it, I knew it! I knew you were doing something stupid. God, you're such a…"

Crab turned her to face him before she found the word she was searching for, and talked to her like a kindly mentor. "Go back to the box, if there's any chance at all of running out of champagne over the next three hours, order some more, then get on your husband's laptop, and get us five tickets for Paris tonight," he said. "The Donahues will meet us there."

She looked at him disbelieving. Crab shooed her on. She was lost for words. "Go on," he said. "Have it done by the time we get back."

"This isn't… he's got a secret cache, hasn't he? Just tell me, are we celebrating, or drowning our sorrows?"

"Just go," said Crab, laughing. "Don't you want to spend the evening in Paris, drinking and dancing?"

She had no idea what she was supposed to say. She pointed at him, then put her hand to her mouth. "You're..." She took herself in a short circle, then came back to Crab with a question, which she lost as soon as she started to ask it. "You're. You're having me on, right? I'm so uptight, that you're having a joke at the expense of an easy target. That's it. That's what you're doing, isn't it?"

Crab shook his head, and reached out to clutch her to him again. She tried to break away from him after a moment, wiping away an emotional tear on her sleeve as she did. "Then what? Come back and go into hiding?"

Crab laughed, still hanging on to her left hand by her fingers. "You're being melodramatic now. We've just disappeared some rogues from their money," he said. Then added, "And I think I heard Min talking about heading on to Tuscany, after Paris." He slowly released her from his grip, as a parent would to a child, learning to ride a bike. "Just go. We'll be back with you in a few minutes."

He and Min amused themselves alone until the next race was run, and the racing finished for the day. They went to wait at a safe distance from the weighing room, until eventually, Faithful appeared, brushed, and scrubbed and made his way towards them. Crab asked them to wait a moment longer, and eventually, the older man who'd been in their box appeared, and came to join them too.

"Who is that?" asked Min.

"Sir Michael," said Crab. "Lady C's ex. He was sitting as a steward today. I thought it was worth booking a little insurance."

Min swallowed his smile as Sir Michael arrived. Crab introduced him, and he gave Faithful a sober congratulations on his winner, which he accepted with a dip of his head, and a gracious smile. Then they set off across the paddock, as a four, line abreast, heading towards their box. No one spoke.

Gary Boswell headed in their direction, heading towards the weighing room with his empty colours bag. It amused him to see the three protagonists in the company of a steward.

"Ooh, do not pass Go, eh lads?" he said. "Or are you on the wrong side of the fix, like me?"

Crab stopped to reply, and without changing his expression, said, "If I were to tell you the sort of fix we're in, you wouldn't believe me."

A story that could not have been told without:

Gaynor Turnbull
Stuart Nicholson
Carole Slone
Beverley Adams
&
Jim Goldie

A rare clutch of good eggs if ever there was one.

Printed in Dunstable, United Kingdom